Y0-CAS-094

May 2004

For Paulette...
Without you and your support... would I have been here now??? Thank you ...ALWAYS! and
HAPPY RETIREMENT !!!

Love & Luck!
June & Hello

Paulette

Boo!

Believe in Miracles !!!

for Bijou,
and her cat, Marcellou
BJH 🐾

for Brian
JHB

Published by Ballyhoo BookWorks Inc.
P.O. Box 534
Shoreham, NY 11786

Copyright © 1993 by Brian J. Heinz
Illustrations © 2001 by June H. Blair

All rights reserved. No parts of this book may
be reproduced or transmitted in any form or by
any means, electronic or mechanical, including
photocopying, recording, or by any information
storage and retrieval system, without the written
permission of the Publisher, except where
permitted by law, or by reviewers who wish to
quote brief passages.

Library of Congress Cataloging-in-Publication Data

Heinz, Brian J., 1946-
        The alley cat / Brian J. Heinz; June H. Blair, illustrator.
            p. cm.
        Originally published: New York, NY : Delacorte Press, 1993.
        Summary: A scarred and tattered alley cat ventures into the
        dangerous world of the city at night to find food for his
        mate and little ones.
          ISBN 0-936335-05-X -- ISBN 0-936335-06-8 (pbk.)
          [1. Cats--Fiction. 2. Stories in rhyme.] I. Blair, June H.,1949- ill. II. Title.

        PZ8.3.H41344 A1 2002
        [E]--dc21

                                        2001043971

RL: 2.6
Printed in China
January 2002
10 9 8 7 6 5 4 3 2 1

Seething steaming sewer grates-
Heaps of rotted packing crates-

Subways grumble deep beneath
The potholes on the city street.

Arching backs and stretching limbs
Are framed in shadows. Night begins.

Grimy drizzle coats the street
To wet and blacken padded feet.

Beyond the alley, headlights shine.
Beyond the alley, sirens whine

In the world of Alley Cats.

Our hero stands in stockinged feet
With preened red fur and snaggled teeth.

His ears are tattered, torn and scarred,
His muscles tense and lean and hard.

The Black, the Manx, the Dappled Gray
Are also here to hunt their prey.

Lonely soldiers, wretched beasts,
Perched on crumpled trash can seats.

Rats are skulking everywhere,
Mice are darting here and there

In the world of Alley Cats.

An iron door groans in the night
And throws out shafts of blinding light

That cut the alley like a knife.
It must be...Yes! The butcher's wife.

A monstrous woman thick of brow
With shoulders broader than a cow.

She squints through cold, unfeeling eyes,
Her thick hands heave the tasty prize.

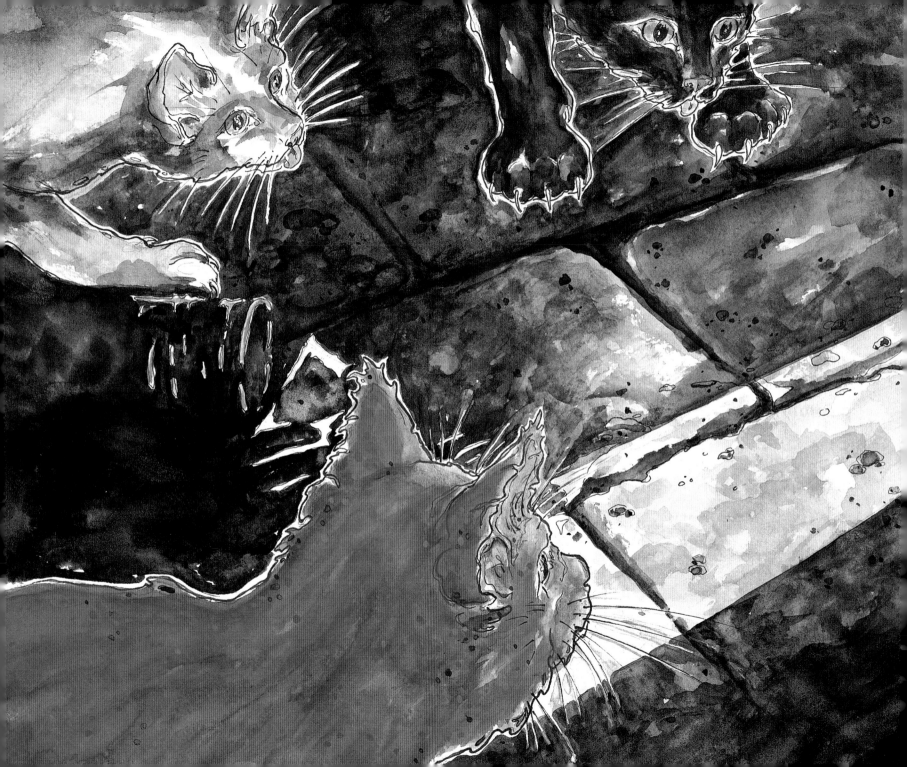

She's gone. The pork chop strikes the ground and
All is still. There's not a sound

In the world of Alley Cats.

Calico stares in deadly silence.
Big Red is up and poised for violence.

They crouch. They stalk. They circle 'round
As bellies brush across the ground.

Our hero lunges at his foe.
Red strikes, and whirls upon his toe.

In tangled turns they rip out hair
Like furry corkscrews in the air.

They writhe and roll and skip and skittle,
Hiss and spit and bleed... a little,

In the world of Alley Cats.

Calico has failed the test,
A limping, sore, bedraggled mess.

They might be friends tomorrow night,
But meat is scarce, they had to fight.

The audience now steals away,
The Black, the Manx, the Dappled Gray.

Our hero proudly claims his prize
And struts about with glowing eyes.

Moonbeams drifting into town
Light Red's path. He's homeward bound

In the world of Alley Cats.

He races under warehouse eaves,
A whirlwind kicking scattered leaves.

Painted scrawls across the wall
Of broken bricks about to fall -

And there! The broken window pane.
He leaps - And he is home again.

Outside? Danger fills the air.
Outside? Yes, life's quite unfair.

But in this dim and musty place
Red sees a soft, familiar face

In the world of Alley Cats.

No claws, no fangs, no need for fear,
His little ones and mate live here.

The Tabby licks his matted hair,
She nuzzles him with loving care.

He purrs and curls up close beside her.
His heart is glad, this brave provider.

Here's his pack of mewling kittens
Dressed in stripes and small white mittens.

He cuffs them gently, one by one,
Three lovely daughters, two fine sons.

Beyond gray walls the night winds moan.
They're not afraid. They're not alone

In the world of Alley Cats.